Dot

by Bobby Lynn Maslen
pictures by John R. Maslen

Scholastic Inc.

New York • Toronto • London • Auckland • Sydney • Mexico City • New Delhi • Hong Kong • Buenos Aires

Beginning sounds for Book 3:

O o — octopus
H h — hat
G g — goat
R r — rabbit

Ask for Bob Books at your local bookstore, or visit www.bobbooks.com.

ISBN 0-439-17547-X

12 11 10   13 14 15/0

Printed in China   68
This edition first printing, May 2006

Dot has a hat.

Dot has a cat.

The cat has a hat.

Dot has a dog. Dog has a ha

Dog has a rag hat.

Sad dog.

Sad Dot. Sad cat.

Dog has on a rag hat.

The End

Available Bob Books®:

Set 1: Beginning Readers
Set 2: Advancing Beginners
Set 3: Word Families
Set 4: Complex Words
Set 5: Long Vowels